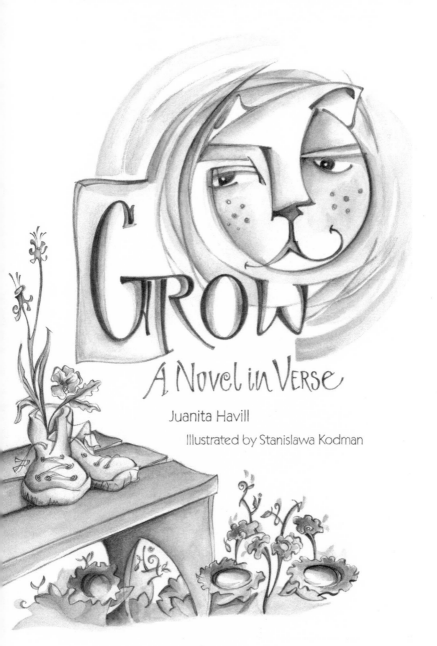

GROW

A Novel in Verse

Juanita Havill

Illustrated by Stanislawa Kodman

PEACHTREE

ATLANTA

Published by
PEACHTREE PUBLISHERS
1700 Chattahoochee Avenue
Atlanta, Georgia 30318-2112
www.peachtree-online.com

Book and cover design by Stanislawa Kodman and Loraine M. Joyner
Composition by Melanie McMahon Ives

Printed in the United States of America
10 9 8 7 6 5 4 3 2 1
First Edition

Library of Congress Cataloging-in-Publication Data

Havill, Juanita.
  Grow / written by Juanita Havill. -- 1st ed.
     p. cm.
  Summary: Two misfit children and other members of a Minneapolis,
Minnesota, neighborhood are brought together by a woman creating
a community garden.
  ISBN 13: 978-1-56145-441-9 / ISBN 10: 1-56145-441-9
  [1. Gardening--Fiction. 2. Community gardens--Fiction.
3. Neighborhood--Fiction. 4. Minnesota--Fiction. 5. Novels in verse.]
I. Title.
  PZ7.S.H42Be 2008
  [Fic]--dc22
  2007029745

To the Berneethas of the world, with gratitude and admiration.

—J. H.

Many people have helped me grow this book.
I would like to thank them for their advice,
encouragement, and support. Some are gardeners,
some not, but all have enriched my life. Thank you to
Emilie Buchwald, Polly Carlson-Voiles, Judy Dyl,
Barbara Joan Flanagin, Elaine Larson, Carol Martin,
Ellen Palestrant, Marge Pellegrino, Lisa Peters,
Charline Profiri, Susan Ray, Claudine Solseng,
Karyn Solseng, and Jan Steinmark.

I am deeply grateful to my editor
Kathy Landwehr, efficient and gentle weeder
with a sense of humor and vision.

Berneetha at the Door

Saturday morning
Berneetha's voice booming
through the screen door
on the front porch:
"I'm all fired up
and ready to go.
Who'll come with me?"
I open the door shouting,
"Me! Where to?"
Red overalls,
blue bandana
over henna-red hair,
and a white T-shirt.
That's Berneetha,
older than my mom,
looking like the Fourth of July,
and it barely being May,

wanting to borrow a rake,
hoe, shovel, and me.
Mom says, "Okay."
She does most times,

6   especially when it means
exercise and burning calories
the way cleaning up
the lot on the corner will.
Berneetha's got big plans.
(No surprise.)
Everything about Berneetha is big—
big belly, big heart, big plans.
This time it's a garden
gonna be blooming
by the end of summer
on Fifth and Vine—
old Mr. Conn's
empty lot,
and he says okay.

I pack a lunch,
set it on the counter.
Now where to find
the landlord's shovel?
I look in the garage
and there it is,
with a hoe, too,
hardly ever used.

"Now, Darlene,
how about a rake
to go with Kate,
and you come, too?"
"Too busy—sorry."
Mom shakes her head
all the way
to the kitchen,
comes back with my lunch.

Later I find out
she took the two devil's food
cookies from my lunch box,
gave me carrots instead.

8

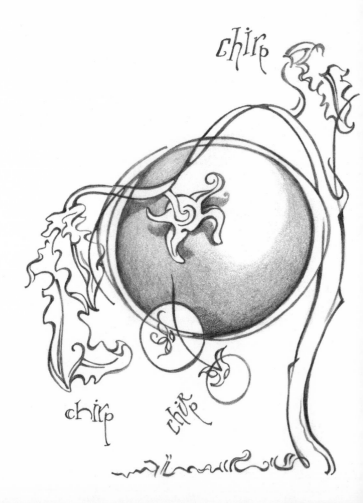

chirp

chirp chirp

About Berneetha

chirp

chirp

chirp

chirp

Mean, I think
when I hear some people
call Berneetha fat.
She's not fat;
she's big.
She's round.
There's a lot of her.
Berneetha's not meant to fit
in the same skinny space
reserved for people
who care about those things.
She's strong, too,
and she's smart.
She used to be a teacher
till they closed down her classroom
to send all the special kids
she taught
someplace else.

No money, no class,
which in a way I'm glad about
'cause now she's got
way more time for me.

Secretly I think
but don't tell her
that some of her kids don't miss her.
I've been to her class,
seen the kids.
Some of them didn't know
who the teacher was,
or where they were.
When I walked in,
they didn't say "yo" or "what's up?"
Or "who are you?"
the way most kids would
if a visitor showed up.

About Berneetha,
she grows things:
catnip, mushrooms,
parsley, crystals,
avocado, tomato,
grapefruit, penicillin.
One time she grew an oak tree
from a seedling
she'd dug out of a wide crack
in a broken sidewalk
and planted it in the park.
Because "Oak trees need space."—
Berneetha's words—
"We all do."

She collects things:
buttons,
bottle caps,
beer steins,
river water in little bottles,

feathers, marbles,
and one hundred and twenty-three
recipes for cheesecake.

12   Berneetha knows things:
how to cure hiccups
by putting a spoon
in a glass of water
and staring at it
while you hold
your breath and sip;
the names of all
the American presidents
and anyone who was
ever governor
of Mississippi, Illinois,
or Minnesota;

where to find blackberries
in the middle of town
in June
and pick them
without getting chigger bites.

She does things:
sizzling, stirring,
zapping, rocking,
purring, jumping
dancing things.
With Berneetha
everything happens
big time
even the quiet things
like sitting still
and staring at frost
on the window in winter
or counting cricket chirps
when the summer sun sets

or staying up past midnight
searching the sky
with binoculars
to get a look
at a comet
as it travels
past Planet Earth
for its once-in-my-lifetime
visit.
Hello, comet!

What I like most
is going over to Berneetha's
and finding out
what's up.

Berneetha's Cats

Thirteen cats share Berneetha.
SamiSue, Groaner, Pumpkin, Ishkar,
Solo,
Albert, Ada, Aberdeen,
He-man, Ozone, Troller, Tough,
and Bo.
She's their human.
They slink through her house,
perch where they want,
eat, sleep, stretch, sleep.
They make me think of seals,
sunning themselves on Berneetha's
slabs of furniture,
except they don't bark like seals.
They are the kind of cats
who stare at you
when you talk to them,

the kind who decide for themselves
whether or not to talk.
Once I knocked
on the door, went in

before Berneetha opened,
the way she tells me to, no big thing,
and SamiSue floored me
with a mother-of-the-house look,
yellow eyes glaring,
waiting for me to ask,
"Can Berneetha come out and play?"
keeping me wondering
what that cat sees
when she looks into my eyes.

The First Day

It's just Berneetha
and me
and SamiSue
standing in the empty lot
on the corner
of Fifth and Vine.
We're the only ones
not too busy
to do something different.

I stare at the empty bottles,
brittle scraps of newspaper,
dried weeds,
dirt and rubble.
"No time for brooding, Kate.
Let's get going
and clean this lot."

"Right," I say. "Clean the dirt?"
"The dirt's the only thing
that's okay," says Berneetha.
"We gotta clear the rubbish.

Wowee, what a mess
some people make!"
Thinking out loud,
I say to Berneetha,
"It's gonna take forever."
"Kate,"—she's getting annoyed—
"didn't you ever hear
Rome wasn't built in a day?
And the Erie Canal?
How long do you think it took
to dig that ditch?
I like a challenge!"

People

People watch us some days,
sideways-like they glance
out of the corners
of their eyes
as if they were too busy
to just stop and stare
and maybe ask us,
"What are you doing
on that lot?"
I guess it takes them
more than a week
to get used to us.
This morning
one man says
loud enough
for everybody walking by
to hear:

"There's that crazy fat lady
who painted her house purple.
Ought to do something
about her."

And I want to tell him
what he ought to do
is grab a shovel
or a rake
and help out
instead of criticizing.
If purple bothers him,
he ought to see
Berneetha's lime green
bathroom
and the big orange zinnia
she painted on the kitchen wall

and all thirteen cats
and the bottle collection
in her fireplace room—
no fire ever, just a big old
log that she switches on

so it looks like it's burning—
and in every one of those bottles:
water,
(muddy brown, pond green,
icy-stream clear),
from one of the rivers,
lakes, streams, or ponds
Berneetha's stuck her toes in
since she was eleven.

I know that man
doesn't have a room full of rivers
so who is he to criticize?

22 "Say, Mr. Harmon,
why don't you put your sneakers on
and come help?"
Berneetha's voice cool
as a fountain,
and I see the man called Mr. Harmon
quit frowning
for an instant
before he walks away.

Help!?

Just one quick eyeball
of those two boys
and I knew
they weren't coming
to help.
Gangstas or wannabes
floating in blue-jean
barrels,
T-shirts like paint-splattered sails.
One tossed stones
pinging
over our heads
against a building
as if we weren't there
hoeing the neatest rows
this side of Iowa

and dropping in seeds
for a bountiful bouquet
of zinnia, cosmos, snapdragon,
sweet pea splendor.

"You two wanna help?"
(Berneetha, of course.)
I edge closer to her,
not feeling comfortable.

"Let's go, Harlan.
We got better things to do."
Harlan,
skinny as a stray cat,
jams his spray paint can in his pocket,
takes in the scene.
Now why did Berneetha
have to go and ask
the graffiti gangstas to help?
I'm thinking Harlan won't stay.
Good.

Berneetha: "See that skinny one,
name of Harlan?
He'll be back."
"Yeah right," I say.
"At night."
And I go cold
worrying they'll wreck
all the good things
we've done in the garden
all day.

Supper

I hold the front door open and say,
"I can't come tonight."
Berneetha, suddenly
as sad as me,
walks off,
turning round to say,
"If things work out,
you come."
I don't tell her
it's 'cause I have to go sit
in the bathroom
on the lid of the toilet
and think about "fat"
and why I ate two little slivers—
all right,
two big pieces—
of a frozen chocolate cake

Mom left on the counter
to thaw out for dessert.
"Hungry!" Mom threw at me
like a pop fly.

"You gonna find out
what hungry means."
While Mom and Jake,
the janitor, "just a friend"
from down the street,
eat pizza, coleslaw—
no, not the slaw
that Mom always orders for me,
made with vinegar,
no cream or mayo
because of the calories—
and yes, chocolate cake,
I sit in the bathroom
looking at everything
but my face in the mirror:

green splotch of toothpaste
hard as paint,
the spider leg poking
out under the mirror
then finally

my brown eyes
(Berneetha says "hazel")
in my face
round as a basketball
my freckles and my tangled hair
that needs combing
and then I see
a splotch of chocolate
at the corner of my mouth
and I reach out with my tongue,
past my lips,
and lick it off—
supper.

Weeds

Turns out
Harlan's good with the rented tiller,
a natural urban farmer.
So it's the three of us now
with SamiSue
after school,
Saturdays, Sundays.
A whole plowed field
is what we have,
and wiry little green shoots
poking through the dirt.
Some of them are weeds
and we pull them in the rain.
The hard part
is figuring out
which are the shoots
we want to grow

and which ones show up
without being invited
like the bad fairy in "Sleeping Beauty."
Harlan has a thing about weeds:

"Weeds have got rights, too."
"Are you kidding?"
I'm being difficult.
"You think we ought to just
grow a whole garden
full of weeds?"
He thinks maybe
a little patch of weeds, anyway.
And Berneetha says,
"I don't see why not.
They were here first.
No harm in sharing."
In the garden book
Berneetha gave me,
I read that weeds
can be anything,

even beautiful flowers,
or beans growing in cornfields.
A weed is anything growing
where you don't want it to grow.
I don't know

where Harlan lives,
only that he looks hungry most days
and he doesn't want
to go home in the evening.
I don't think I'll tell him
about that garden-book
theory of weeds.

Witness

At the garden early,
my hands full of weeds,
I hear a voice holler,
"Got the manure lined up!"
I look up,
first thing I see:
Berneetha beaming
as she marches across the street,
a drum major
leading a parade.
"Guaranteed delivery right to the garden."
Then half a block behind her
comes SamiSue,
slithering one moment,
prancing the next
in that proud panther gait.

Next,
Harlan in a panic run,
shirt and pants flopping
as he pounds around the corner,

dives behind the juniper thicket.
Last thing I see:
a blue Chevy low-rider truck
wobbles two-wheeled
around the corner,
brakes screeching,
and pops onto the curb
at the very same moment
in the very same spot
SamiSue had picked out
for herself.

My stomach hollow with pain,
I watch the black cat's body
roll over and over,
land limp
behind the juniper,

and I stand there
staring
at what I don't want to see
while the blue hit-and-run
backs off the curb
and speeds away.

Harlan crawls out
and his scream
has the power of pain
times three.
Loud enough for all of us.

Funeral

No way
am I going to tell Berneetha,
"At least you've got
twelve more cats"
to make her feel better.
Berneetha has her own brand of love
for each cat,
not "cat love" in an amount
that fits all.
I can see the empty place
in her eyes—
empty that can't be filled up
with any old cat.

Harlan brushes off his jeans.
I wipe my soggy cheeks.
Together we dig
a deep, deep hole
in the middle of the garden.
Then it's time.
At the bottom of the hole
SamiSue lies still,
a ruby of blood at her nostril.
We drop handfuls of dirt
until she disappears.
Berneetha piles rocks
on the grave.

Not knowing what to do,
I start humming the song
the preacher's daughter
sang at my grandma's funeral.
Then Berneetha, looking
like an anvil crushed

her soul,
starts singing,
"He walks with me,
and he talks with me..."
Harlan hums and I sing

a word or two I know
while Berneetha's voice
vibrates with some kind of emotion,
whether joyful or sorrowful
I can't say,
maybe both,
and I know that wherever she is,
SamiSue can hear Berneetha
and feel her love.

When I climb the porch steps,
all dragging and heavy,
Mom says to me,
"You've been crying."
And I tell her what happened.

Softly, almost sweet,
her voice, as she tries
to reassure me:
"Berneetha's got

at least
a dozen more cats.
It's not as if
she doesn't have any."

Call Me "Chitra"

Dr. Arockiasamy strolls up
to talk about tomatoes.
She used to live
around here
but now she only
comes once a week
to work at the clinic
at Seventh and Vine.
All danger of frost is past,
the doctor tells us,
and she's been waiting
and watching

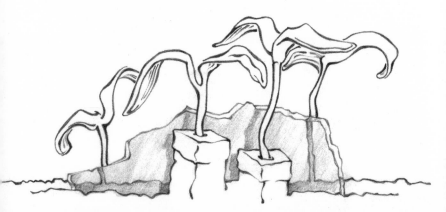

and if someone—
she looks at me
and Harlan—
is willing,

44

she has two big flats
of tomato seedlings
down at the clinic.
"Thank you, Dr. Arockiasamy,
we do appreciate it."
"Call me Chitra," she says,
surprising me, but why?
Did I think that her first name
was "doctor"?

Chitra wanders around
the garden
to find the perfect spot
for twenty-four tomato plants
that Harlan and I carry,
one flat each,

staring at the lacy leaves
with their fuzz of weensy white hairs.
We all of us—me, Berneetha, Harlan,
Chitra on her knees in the dirt—
plant the seedlings.
Chitra smooths the dirt
around each stem.
"They're going to love it here."
Berneetha quick with her invitation:
"Come back soon.
You be in charge of tomatoes, Chitra."
"I can handle that."
Chitra grins and "good-byes"
and says, "Keep your shoes on, Kate."
We both laugh
and I have to explain
to Harlan what Berneetha already knows,

how
when I was eight
I stepped on broken glass
and Dr. Arockiasamy
sewed up the slit
in my heel.
It was numb, of course,
and I watched her
make neat little stitches
in my skin
and close the gap.
And Mom said,
"Don't you watch.
It'll make you sick
to your stomach."
But it didn't bother me.
Then the nurse
gave me a tetanus shot
and I threw up.

My Dad

The day the check came
Mom took me shopping.
"For once your dad
got his act together.
We won't see another
one of these babies
for a long time."

All I remember
about my dad
is him yelling at Mom
and her yelling at him.
And one other thing—
this goes way back,
to a Sunday
he took me swimming.

I was maybe four
and climbed
up the bright red ladder
of the water slide

and stared,
way too scared
to move,
so he came right
up the ladder
and put me
on his lap,
and we flew down
to splash
at the bottom,
but he held me up
so my head
didn't go under.
Then he left.

After that
I had to hold
my head up
by myself.

49

Going Shopping

Mom buys herself
a slinky orange blouse
and big white dangly
hoop earrings.
"Think summer, Kate."

I think overalls,
but she picks out
a frilly skirt
and a purple tank top
that I take to a stall
with a chipped chair
and a torn green curtain.
I'm thinking my bulges
are all in the wrong places.

I twirl, just once,
and the skirt floats
like a parachute
then drapes
and tickles my knees.

"Kate? Kate?
Does it fit?"

I bite my lip,
unpeel the top,
slip the skirt
over my hips.

In my baggy jeans again
I ignore Mom's frown,
hand her the items.
"They fit."
"Let's take them."
We both win.

Mr. Wasserman

"Jacob," he tells me.
"Call me Jacob."
Burly man,
chest like a propane tank,
curly silver whiskers,
thick round glasses,
he's always frowning
(so I thought).
Berneetha's been every day
looking over her shoulder,
waiting, never doubting,
then today,
mid-June,
he finally shows up
in a noisy pickup truck,
hauling a load of manure.

Mr. Wasserman points his thumb
at the driver.
"My nephew tells me
his cows don't mind
how much I take.
Manure makes for happy plants."

I think something about the manure
must tickle Harlan's funny bone
'cause he grins so wide
you can count all his teeth,
and that's when it happens:
Jacob Wasserman smiles back.

He dumps the manure,
stays to help Berneetha
spread it nice and even;
comes back the next day
to help build teepee towers
for the snap beans.
"Sarah used to grow beans."

Berneetha
points to green tendrils twisting
on smooth earth mounds.
"You'll know what to do then."

Sarah?
I never saw her,
and I've been here twelve years.
"Wife?" I whisper to Berneetha.
"Daughter," she says softly.
"Cancer."

Harlan's Favorite Flowers

It was Berneetha's idea
to plant pansies,
the Johnny-jump-up kind,
in the shade
at the foot
of the garden bed
like a folded quilt.
It's Harlan
who takes to the dinky flowers
like they were some kind
of security blanket.
One morning I catch him early,
see him kneeling
beside the pansies,
reaching out to touch
the velvet petals.

I stop still,
don't say a word,
let Harlan be with his pansies.
I can almost hear his brain
thinking out loud,
"Cool."

Once he asked Berneetha
how a whole plant
can sprout and grow and flower
all from a sliver of seed.
What was it
in that seed
that made it grow
in the dirt
and bloom yellow, white,
purple, orange, maroon,
like a conjure man had spoken
a spell over it?

Berneetha said
we all start as seeds—
each of us different,
each of us beautiful.

Harlan hears me
sneaking up on him.
Does he know I'm listening
to his noisy brain?
He turns.
I see a purple swollen bruise
on his chocolate cheek
and a scab on his busted lip.

We all start as seeds
growing in dirt.
And Berneetha says
something else too:
Each of us
has something to be proud of.

Back When I Was Ten

On the way home from the garden
Harlan walks a ways with me,
till we come to the fire station.

I used to have a crush
on one of the firefighters,
Tony Donatello,
with his black hair,
black eyes, easy smile.
He teased me about
my orange hair
going every which way,
and he would let me
and Becky and Josephina
help him polish the fire engine
on Saturdays in the summer,
before Becky and Josephina's

mom and dad did something so terrible
Becky and Josephina had to go
away to live someplace else.
We used to play baseball, too,
in the empty lot
beside the fire station.

Tony ambles out,
asks if we have something to do,
and Harlan looks down, all around,
mumbles, "I gotta go,"
and runs off like a stray dog
that's been yelled at.
I say to Tony, "I guess not,"
wondering what it was
about Tony
that spooked Harlan,
wondering if I'd outgrown
that little-kid crush—

because polishing a big red truck
wasn't first anymore
on my list
of things to do.

63

Adam, Aaron, Abe

The Simpson brothers—
Adam, the second grader,
Aaron in first,
Abe starts kindergarten
in the fall—
come to the garden
with a little blue plastic bucket.
"To water the flowers,"
Aaron says.

"Why thank you very much."
Berneetha turns the faucet
to let water pour
into the blue bucket
from our big water tank—

so big it takes
both Berneetha and me
to pull it on the wagon
when it's full.

No matter that Berneetha
shows them
the right way to water,
Adam runs up and down the rows
Aaron dribbles water
on the eggplant seedlings,
and Abe stands and stares.
As soon as the bucket is empty,
they say they have to go.
You just know
the only reason
they showed up
was to find out
what was going on.
It doesn't take three boys
to carry a little bucket.

Afro-Caribbean *Macbeth* Witch

I believe Berneetha
when she tells me,
"I was an actress once—
and a dancer on the stage."
She mops sweat
from her face
with an orange scarf,
sits down on the garden bench,
gift of Monika Schroeder,
whose brother works
at a hardware store.
I watch the space
between the slats
grow wider
and wonder
if Berneetha leans back
or takes a deep breath,
will the boards hold?

She jumps up,
shrinking the space.
"Yes sir, I was dancing
one of the three voodoo

witches in a 500-year-old
play by Mr. William Shakespeare,
Macbeth,
the Scottish play,
all about a wannabe king
who goes and murders the real king,
but this was
the Afro-Caribbean version,
all song and dance,
and the three witches,
one of them being me,
danced around a cauldron
on the stage
of that little cramped theater
across the river in St. Paul."

Talk about impressed.
The only play
I've been to
is *Arsenic and Old Lace*
in the church basement—
murder, sure,
it's a mystery,
but no cauldron, no witches,
and no dancing, no way.

Wild Dancing

Berneetha's body's moving.
She shakes, sways,
stamps her garden boots
to the rhythm
of a witch's chant:
"Eye of newt and toe of frog.
Wool of bat and tongue of dog.
Double, double toil and trouble.
Fire burn and cauldron bubble."
Her body swings,
swoops, spins.
Her arms trace circles.
Harlan drops his rake
and starts clapping,
then stamps
and spins
and I jump in.

We make it up as we go along.
Anyone walking by
will think we're crazy people
for sure,

wild-dancing in the garden.
We are actors.
We are dancers.
Why should we care
what they think?

Hank Glover and Otis McGuire

Hank wants to plant corn.
Mom says he looks older
than he is
because of the war.
He was a soldier,
and every time I see him now
his hands are shaking,
but I don't know
if that's because of the war
or if he has Parkinson's
like Great-Grandma McGregor
and is bad sick.

Sometimes Otis pushes him
in a wheelchair.
Berneetha says they're
kind of married,
Hank and Otis,

and that makes me wonder,
but when my thoughts go there,
I get mixed up.
All I know about

74

marriage is
divorce.

The Death of Randall Conn

Berneetha sees the post first
and on the post
a notice.
"Hearing?"
She reads the word
like a question
so I ask,
"Hearing?"
"Yes, Little Miss Echo—
hearing.
To talk about rezoning
so they can build a parking garage
in the middle of our garden.
When they're through,
won't be a garden left."

Side by side
we stare at the paper
on the post.
Seems the members

of the city council—
mind you,
people who have never
seen fit
to set foot
in our garden,
let alone,
plow, dig, weed, or plant in it—
are wanting to have a meeting
to talk about
what *they're* going to do with
our garden.

July 1
10:30 a.m.
City Hall
Minneapolis.

Why did Randall Conn
have to die?
And his son Herbert
come along with dollars in his eyes?
Instead of our garden
he sees a parking garage
four stories high?
"He can't do that, can he?"
I see fire in Berneetha's eyes.
"Not without a fight."

Jackpot

I count the daisies
before we leave:
thirty-six happy-face
sunshine flowers.
Will they bring us luck?
"We need more than luck, Kate.
We need to keep
our wits about us.
We need guts
to say what we think
and fill the chambers
with arguments
about how the good things
we're doing
would be even better
if Mr. Conn would just give
the garden one summer

to grow and bloom
and be so beautiful,
then he might
change his mind

and let the garden grow
like his dad did.
We need time
to line up the neighbors,
make sure each one shows up
at the back of the courtroom
holding up signs:
Save Our Soil
Be Kind to Plants
Gardens Are Forever,
helping the commissioners
see the truth:
Where would we all be without places
for plants to grow in peace?"

Berneetha shifts gears.
The engine of her rusty, red Civic
whines.
Harlan in the backseat
lets out a yell

that makes my eardrum throb.
"2-0-0-0-0-0!
Do you see it?
Just now,
like a jackpot
on your speedometer,
Berneetha.
It's a sign.
It means good luck."
Berneetha smiles,
shakes her head and says,

"Since we don't have
200,000 quick-witted,
gutsy garden lovers
all with boom box voices

pleading our case,
maybe luck will do us some good."

Day in Court

Finally the doors open,
frosted glass in lacquered
black wood.
Berneetha, Harlan, me—
the first to arrive—we
take our places
up front.
"At least
another half hour."
Clerk looks down her nose
at people
who don't know
what time they're supposed
to come to the court.
Harlan fidgets,
looks over his shoulder
and every which way.

"I don't like
this place.
You come here
to get something taken away."
"200,000, Harlan.
Did you forget?"
My voice so loud
the clerk clears her throat
and shushes me
with an evil-eye stare.
I look down,
feeling the heat
in my cheeks
and knowing how red they are.
I try to think myself
somewhere else
and remember a book
my mom has on the table
by her bed:
THE POWER OF POSITIVE THINKING

When I asked her what it was about,
she said, "Read it sometime.
It's about
making good things happen
because you turn your brain on
to what you want.
Long as what you want is good,
you get it."
I tried for a while,
thinking myself
twenty-five pounds thinner.
For a good cause—
not for me,
for my mom.
But nothing happened.
After all of that thinking,
I wasn't even one pound lighter.

Sitting here,
I wish
I'd read
Mr. Norman Vincent Peale's book,
just for some know-how
so maybe I could do it right.
Berneetha has so many
wrinkles in her forehead,
I don't think
even positive thinking
will iron them out.
We sit quiet
like rabbits
in a hawk's shadow
for what seems like an hour,
afraid that lady
will shush us again.
Then the doors swing
wide.

Over my shoulder,
I see
Mr. Wasserman
holding the doors open,
leading

Chitra,
Hank Glover,
Otis McGuire,
and people
I've seen around
but I don't know
their names.
Neighbors.
A whole crowd of them—
no accident—
squeezing through the door,
filling the room
like the cavalry
in the nick of time.
I can almost
hear the bugles.

Shortcake

I stare at the strawberry shortcake
towering on a plate
in front of me
and I do something
I have never done:
let my spoon dangle
and stare, just stare
at dessert.

"Kate, what's got into you?
Turning up your nose
at my shortcake
like there's bugs in the berries,
or poison in the whipped cream.
You must be sick."

"Mad," I say,
"too mad to eat."

She says, "Nothing
you can do
about Mr. Conn's plans."

I snap my head up, shoot a look at her.
"Don't tell me it's his land,
and he can do whatever:
send out heavy
trucks to scrape
and blade,
pay the concrete pourers,
the carpenters,
bricklayers, and window hangers,
anybody he wants
to bury the snapdragons,
hollyhocks, cosmos,

tomatoes, and zucchini
under slabs of cement
for a bunch of cars
to park their butts on.

"Don't tell me
that garden belongs to
somebody who never
dug a hole
or planted a seed,
'cause if it does,
Mom, if that garden
belongs to Mr. Conn,
then why even
bother to go to the hearing
'cause nothing's fair
in the whole city.
Land ought to belong
to the people
who care about it."

Mom's eyes sparkle
with common sense.
She is going to wrap
me up in common sense
and make me feel better.

92

"Kate, how would you feel
if you planted a garden
and Mr. Conn came along
with plans for a building
on the same land
'cause he says a building is better
than a garden any day
even if it's your land
bought and paid for?
You'd want your garden,
wouldn't you,
same as he wants his building now."

"No fair, Mom."
"Don't sass me, Kate."

I am quiet now
hearing in my head
what Berneetha said,
"The hearing's over
but we're not done yet."

Night

A sliver of moon.
I toss and turn.
The air is so heavy
it makes car engines
rumble like thunder,
so sticky
it catches up the cricket chirps
and won't let them fall to the ground.

I wish I could sleepwalk.
Anyone catches me,
they'd leave me alone,
afraid to wake a sleepwalker.
But I'm wide awake
when I sneak out the door
and shadow leap
down the street

to the garden
and sit on stones
beside the cosmos
glowing yellow in the streetlight.

If I sit here
when the trucks come,
and refuse to move,
will they run over me?

What's that?
I jump at a noise,
skitter like a graffiti artist
caught in the act
with a can of spray paint.
Quiet again.
I breathe.
Some courageous protestor
I'll be,
scared to be alone

in the garden at night.
Pepper plants shake
in the shadows.
I hear scratching in the dirt
a squirrel?—
and I cringe.
"Harlan, is that you?"
Wishing I'd kept
my mouth shut
the minute I speak.
What if it's Mr. Conn's men
coming at night to steal
the garden?
But why come at night
when it's so easy
to steal it fair and square
in court
in the middle of the day?

The moon is gone.
I walk home in darkness
but not so dark
that I don't see Tony Donatello
heading toward
the fire station.
I crouch behind a car
and wonder why
he stops two blocks from the station
and wanders into our garden
at night.

Secrets

Berneetha's up to something—
the way she raises
her eyebrows
and smiles with her lips
together,
not a big-toothed
Berneetha smile.

"What's up?" I ask.
I plead
but Berneetha won't tell,
says maybe I
ought to thin
the tomato plants
all by myself
until Harlan shows up

'cause she's off
to talk to someone
about something
and won't tell
no matter how I beg.

100

"What if your mom
ordered you
a mountain bike
to surprise you
for your thirteenth birthday,
but then she
went and told you
all about it?
You wait and wait,
getting excited,
ready to explode,
then on the day,
it doesn't show up.

Nothing she can
give you now
will make it right."

So Berneetha's got

a point
but I'm not
a little kid anymore.
Anyway why would
my mom think
about giving me
a mountain bike
when I have
a perfectly decent
secondhand ten-speed
with three of the gears
still working?

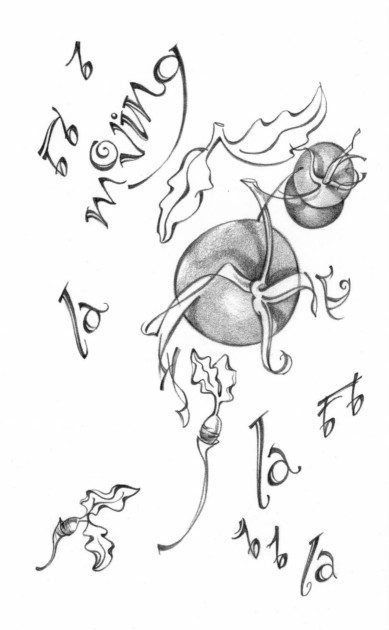

My Hero

Tony Donatello Tony
Donatello Tony
Donatello
says we're
gonna move the garden gonna
move the garden gonna
move the garden.
He's my hero he's my Tony
Donatello he's my Tony
Donatello.

moving

Moving Day

If plants had feet
instead of roots
and hands instead
of stems and leaves,
we could take each one
by the hand,
lead the tomatoes, radishes,
sweet peas, pumpkin seedlings,
and all the flowers
down the street:
"Look before you cross,"
we'd remind them
and squeeze their little hands
if they got rambunctious
and tried to run ahead,
or if they shook with fear
about moving to a new lot

even though they were heading
for fresh-dug,
warm, wet, welcoming plots
in the empty lot

beside the firehouse.
The way I see it,
Chitra leads the tomatoes,
Harlan carries the pansies,
Berneetha watches
out for the sunflowers
and tells the pumpkins to behave.
"Now don't complain.
It's only a short walk."
A regular parade of plants
marching down the sidewalk.

"This would be a lot easier
if the plants hadn't gone and
grown so big."
Harlan breaks the spell.

We laugh and
I look back
to see Monika Schroeder
carrying a rake
and a coil of hose
over her shoulder
and behind her
SURPRISE:
my mom
with a red apron
over her housedress
and her arms
around a plastic tub
of eggplants,
their leaves drooping.
"They probably won't make it,"
she tells me,
"but you gotta try."

Transplanting

I remember—
this morning
before we moved
the garden—
how Berneetha looked
over her shoulder
at SamiSue's grave,
no time to linger.
I saw her eyes stare,
her forehead wrinkle,
and the little nod she gave
to shake herself
back to business,
and right then
I made a plan—
which is why
Harlan and me
are in the garden tonight,

whispering
so our voices
won't echo
across the empty lot.

"Here's where we buried her."
I pull my gloves on
and beam the flashlight
on the little pile of rocks,
stoop to pick them up.
"Are you sure?"
Harlan shakes his head.
"I mean,
are you sure
you want to dig up a dead cat?"

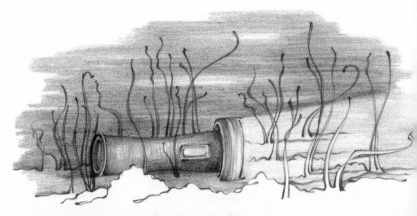

"I'm sure
that SamiSue belongs
in the garden
not under some parking lot."

But I know
what he's thinking:
skeleton,
rotting body,
worms.
That's why I brought
the box from my old ice skates,
big enough
for a stiff skeleton.

We're good at digging—
ought to be,
we dig all day every day.
Over a foot down,

I hit something soft.
Harlan beams the light,
dirt all over the fur,
one eye missing.
I close both of mine,
and feel-dig
until I can scoop under,
lift her out,
into the box
that Harlan closes quick,
before my curiosity
can make me peek
to see what a cat
been buried for six weeks
looks like.

It's SamiSue.
Let her rest in peace.

"My dad done it.
He killed SamiSue."

What is Harlan talking about?
Suddenly I'm thinking
about the blue truck
and Harlan running,
and I,
who do not usually
have trouble talking,
get a lump in my throat.

"I hate him,"
Harlan says.
No way am I gonna tell him
that he shouldn't,
because I'm thinking
that I hate Harlan's dad, too,
and I don't even know him.

What Berneetha Says

Berneetha's not
looking at me,
but staring down
at the daisies
Harlan and me
planted over SamiSue's
new resting place.

"I never had a child,
never been married,
but if I did,
I'd be happy, Kate,
if my daughter
was just like you,
or if I had a son
like you, Harlan."

I bend down
to brush crumbs
of dirt off the leaves.
"Not the neatest
transplant job,"
I mumble.

Harlan clears his throat.
Is he thinking
what I'm thinking?
Those daisies
have got to make it.

Me Singing

Me hurrying home
to fold the laundry.
Me singing, singing
singing all day
with that happy,
warm-goodness
feeling spreading
over my body
like liquid sunshine,
like Christmas in July.

How Does a Sunflower Grow?

Like waiting for a kitten
to grow into a cat,
I know
what sunflowers
are supposed
to look like,
but why does it take
forever?
I know
the little green leaves
will be wide and floppy,
that somehow
a disk will grow
covered with seeds,
black and white
and scrunched together,
and all around the disk
a yellow-petaled halo.

The first time
I look at the sunflower seedling
and see
wiry green shoots
and a green leaf unfurl,
I wonder
how that tiny sprout
will ever grow
into a green giant
six feet tall
with a hundred seeds
and floppy yellow petals
like the picture
on the seed packet,
like Berneetha promised.
So I worry out loud to Berneetha,
"What if it never gets big enough,
never blooms before summer's over?"
"Be patient," she says—

her favorite saying
when it comes to the garden.
"Tell me, Kate,
did you ever look at a baby
all round and messy and fussing
and a day or two later
look again and
wonder why
she wasn't all grown up?"
And I grinned.
"No."
But just then the thought
of Baby Berneetha
pops into my head,
and I can't
keep from smiling
because the baby I see
has a huge round face
like a sunflower disk

and bright brown Berneetha eyes
and she's wearing
a yellow-petaled bonnet.

Later I tell Harlan
about the sunflower face
I saw
in my imagination,
but he doesn't get it,
can't believe
Berneetha was ever a baby.

Bolting Lettuce

Some of the big early tomatoes
are red,
round, and juicy.
Radishes picked
and crunched,
their spicy cool
oozing
in my mouth.
If we give it
half a chance,
the lettuce
will bolt.
(Berneetha's word.)
When she tells me
about bolting,
I think I feel
what the lettuce feels.

People have finally quit
pulling leaves off
here and there,
cutting me down to size.

They let me have my head,
let me grow, grow, grow
into what
I've been wanting
to be all along—
a flower.

A NAME FOR THE GARDEN

The first thing
that pops into my head:
Berneetha's Garden.
Or what about
Berneetha and Tony's
Firehouse Garden?
'Cause without Berneetha,
without Tony,
without the firehouse,
there wouldn't be a garden.
Without me and Harlan, either.
Without Otis and Hank,
Jacob, Chitra, Monika.
Even Adam, Abe, and Aaron
helped—
and can't forget
my mom.

SamiSue
in her own way
she helped, too.
Maybe
the SamiSue Memorial Garden.
No.
Too sad.
This garden
is about happy.
Call it
Happy Garden.

Happy Garden Party

Bubble, bubble,
toil, no trouble,
the brand-new
fountain gurgles
like a happy baby
when Tony plugs in
the motor
and says,
"This is for Berneetha."
Everyone cheers
as if Tony plugged
them in, too,
and Berneetha
is so surprised.
The way I know is
for a whole minute
she stares
at the fountain,

at us,
and she doesn't
say a word!
Then she's crying

and smiling and
"Thank you thank you thank you,
but the fountain
belongs to you,
just like the garden."
Next thing
Berneetha starts hugging,
Tony first,
then me and Harlan,
then Otis and Hank.
My mom gives
her a big hug, too.
Everybody starts
hugging each other.
I hug Harlan
and he hugs me back.

Berneetha's Kids

I'm thinking
I was wrong
about Berneetha's kids—
the ones in her class
when she taught special ed,
the ones
I thought
couldn't know what
was going on—
ever.
Berneetha brought
some of her kids
to see the garden,
dip their fingers
in the fountain,
smell the sweet William,
taste the cherry tomatoes.

In their own minds
in their own way,
maybe they do know
who Berneetha is.

I look at Tara,
the black-haired girl
whose neck can't hold
her head up,
who drools spit
down her chin.
Berneetha crouches
beside the wheelchair
and pops open
a big orange snapdragon.
In Tara's eyes
I see something
that tells me
she knows Berneetha,
that some of
Berneetha's happiness
has rubbed off on her.

After the Garden Party

Harlan's hand
and my hand
together
squeezing
each other
all the way
from the garden
to my house.
We don't talk
'cause it's hard
to hold hands
and talk
at the same time.
Too much
other stuff going on
in your head,
in your stomach.

Then our hands
let go.
"Bye."
"See ya."
And all this stuff
going on
all over.

THE blue TRUCK

Noon and hot.
Time for a break.
Harlan splashes me
with cold fountain water.
I splash him right back.
Berneetha shakes dirt
from her gloves.
"Pick some jalapeños,"
she says.
"I'm off to get us
a deluxe pizza."
She drives off
hollering out the window,
"My treat!"

I'm hoping she remembers
to tell them to
hold the anchovies,

but she's too far now
for me to yell.
She doesn't see the cops
stomp into the garden.

Bad news,
I can tell.
"Harlan Connors?"
The one with sunglasses
speaks first,
his voice so stern
it makes ME feel guilty.
I start shaking.

"We need to talk
about a missing car
and some graffiti, too."

Is Harlan scared?
I don't know.
His eyes dart
from the cops to me—

not mad, not scared,
but let's get it over with.

"Tell Berneetha,"
his voice so low
only I can hear,
"I wouldn't have nuthin'
to do with
stealin' Joe's truck,
not for no drop-offs
for my dad.
Made him so mad
he went joyriding
like a wild man."
Then his voice
gets tight and angry.
"It's my dad
who told the cops—
but it's a lie."

The stolen truck,
a flash of blue—I see it again:
Harlan running,
the truck hitting,

SamiSue rolling
over and over.
"That's crazy," I say
loud enough for
the cops to hear.
How can I make them
go away?
"It wasn't Harlan
driving that truck."
I can't believe I'm yelling
at a cop.
"He was running
down the sidewalk.
How could he be driving?
But I didn't see the driver
'cause I was watching
SamiSue."

The quiet cop—
the one without sunglasses—
focuses his squinty blue
eyes on me,
says, "Maybe this SamiSue
saw the driver?"

"SamiSue is dead," I say.
"You never saw a cat like her—"
All at once I'm bawling,
can't keep from it,
and the cop tells me, "Calm down,"
asks for my name and address
so they can come and talk to me
again

"Let's go, Harlan,"
Sunglasses says.
Harlan comes real close.

It hurts me to look
in his eyes.
"The graffiti on the firehouse—
it was me."

He doesn't have
to say "I'm sorry"
but he does,
and then he's gone.

Harlan's Gone

Nothing my mom
can say
will make me
stop crying.
I hurt everywhere,
my head throbbing,
my heart aching,
my throat choking tight.
Nothing my mom
can say
will make me eat—
normally I would laugh
about my mom
begging me to eat,
but not today.

I keep crying,
a slobbery mess
in a heap on my bed,
alone.

140

Harlan's Back

A witness
is somebody
who sees the truth
like Berneetha and me.
We're witnesses.
If SamiSue
was still alive,
could talk,
could tell us
what she saw that day,
she'd be a witness, too.

Harlan wasn't
driving that truck.
That's part of the truth.
He didn't steal it either.
That's the other part.
The whole truth.

Berneetha saw
a bald white guy
in a black T-shirt
driving the low-rider.

The cops
believe Berneetha
and me, too,
when I say
Harlan was running,
running away from the truck.
Harlan can go home
with Berneetha—
but just until
they find
his grandmother.

So who was
driving the truck?
The cops at the police station
want to know.

Sunglasses (still wearing sunglasses)
holds up photos
of bald white men
until Berneetha taps
a photo. "That's him."

Turns out that bald white guy
in a black T-shirt
is Harlan's dad.
Harlan never told.
Was he that afraid,
or was it something else?

Could I tell
a stranger cop
if my mom did something
bad wrong?
But she wouldn't
so I'll never know.

Harlan's Gone Again

If I had a grandmother
in Chicago
who said,
"Come live with me"
and a mom
who's dead
and a dad
who yells at me
and hits me
in the mouth
and lies about me
to the cops
and who's gone
to jail, anyway,
I'd go
to Chicago
for sure
unless

I could live
with Berneetha.

She tells Harlan
that if things
don't work out
in Chicago,
he's welcome
to come
live with her.
And I'm happy
'cause Berneetha's offering
him a home right here
and trying to be happy
'cause Harlan's
got a grandma,
but when I go home,
halfway happy or not,
I throw myself
on my bed
and cry.

Monday Morning Early

Third week of school
and brrr cold.
I unzip
my winter jacket
from the storage bag
and sniff the mothball smell,
sharp and chemical.
I pull on the jacket
and sneeze twice,
head out for the door.

"Why you leavin'
so early?
What's so important
about gettin'
to the bus stop
at 7 a.m.?"

"I walk slow
in the morning.
That's when I
do my best thinkin'."

"Save some
of that thinkin'
for math class."

"Sure, Mom."
I pull my sock hat
over my ears
to ward off
the not-so-wonderful
surprise of cold.

But it's not just the cold
that takes away
my breath
when I stop by the garden,

but what the cold
did to the garden last night.
Like I was punched in the stomach,
that's how I feel
when I see what that killer frost did.

I never felt this way before
about the grass
turning brown
or the yellow leaves
blowing off the birches
when the weather turned cold.
Maybe 'cause
I never had a garden
before,
something so full
of red, yellow, purple,
orange, white, lavender,
and green, green, green,
overnight gone to brown, black,
wilting, drooping,

given-up-on life,
so shrunken?
The sight
gets me in the gut—
I want to pump
everything up
and spray paint it green.

Then I worry
about the water
in the fountain.
It's gonna freeze
and crack the cement.
With my bare hands
I splash the freezing
fountain water
down on the
circle of Johnny-jump-ups.
Blooming again—
they quit for a while

and went scraggly in the heat—
thick and green-leaved now,
their little velvet faces
turn up to me,
asking for help.

After school
I dig them out,
the helpless pansies,
put them in pots,
and cart them home
in the wagon,
hoping I'm not
too late.

Berneetha at the Door

"Yo, Kate!"
Berneetha's knocking
at the door.
"I'll go, Mom."
I get up
from the floor
beside the pansies
where I've been sitting,
thinking.
I wipe my eyes,
sniff all the way
downstairs to the front door.

"Is some person
here gonna tell me
about the missin' pansies?"

I take Berneetha
upstairs
to my room,
show her where
I put them
beneath the window
where sun pours in
all morning.
Berneetha hugs me.
"That's not the only
reason I'm here."
She's leading me
back to the front door.
"Got my job back!
Money's there
for me and my kids.
Come celebrate with me."

First thing that
comes to mind
is Tara
with her black, black hair
and how happy
she's gonna be.
"How about
we go get
an ice cream sundae?
My treat."
I grab my jacket,
pull my hat
over my ears.
Mom's standing
in the hall.
"Hey, Darlene,
you come, too."

Berneetha's smile
is wide enough
for us all to fit in,
and Mom smiles, too.
"I'll get my coat.
Kinda cold
for ice cream, though.
Don't ya think?"

The Last Poem Is Really the First

I stare at the notebook paper,
thin blue lines
that I'm supposed
to be writing on,
pink up-and-down stripes
to keep me
from scribbling
across the margin.
But we're supposed
to write poems
today—
long lines all the way to and even
across the pink line if we want,
or short lines
if
we
want.

We can write
about now,
or write about yesterday
and make it seem
like now.

I think I'm gonna
like poetry.
I just have to
figure out
what to write about.
I doodle
little loopy circles
in the margin.
The doodle grows
into a big round
sunflower with petals
shooting out like sunbeams
around a sunflower face.

LIGHTBULB!

I'll write about
Berneetha.